RACHEL WEEPS

RACHEL WEEPS

TRAYNOR

ORIGINAL THIRTEEN
Publishing

This book is lovingly dedicated to all mothers, especially those whose arms are empty.

Trigger Warning

This story deals, briefly, with the violent death of a child. If this is too much for you, you can skip chapter two and go straight to chapter three.

Verse

Then Herod, when he saw that he was mocked of the wise men, was exceeding wroth, and sent forth, and slew all the children that were in Bethlehem, and in all the coasts thereof, from two years old and under, according to the time which he had diligently inquired of the wise men.

Then was fulfilled that which was spoken by Jeremiah the prophet, saying:

"In Rama was there a voice heard, lamentation, and weeping, and great mourning, Rachel weeping for her children, and would not be comforted, for they are not."

- Matthew 2:16-18, King James Version

Contents

1

The Messenger

A boy runs through the alley. She can hear him coming long before he rounds the narrow corner, dodging the poorly stacked baskets on one side and the tethered donkeys on the other. He is fast, this boy, and he is strong. He shouts the whole way down the lane.

"He is here! He has come!"

The high, young voice echoes off the tall walls that surround them. The slap-slap-slap of his sandals, freshly made and still stiff, sound like the drums announcing an official. Behind him, a few smaller children run, giggling, excited, giddy with promise.

"He has *come!*"

Dinah leans against the doorway, watching them as they race toward her. She has been working since before dawn this morning, preparing not only for the Sabbath, which is a weekly endurance test in itself, but also for the coming Passover, and she is tired. It is only midday and the clay walls surrounding her have absorbed the heat and kept the interior cool. The sun can't even reach this alleyway, so narrow is this path, yet she is sweating. Tired, sweating, and too wrapped in her thoughts to even scold the children for shouting.

I am old, she thinks, and the thought is both sad and comforting. *I don't know when it happened, but I am old.*

That is a lie. She knows exactly when it happened, down to the minute. But it doesn't bear speaking of. She won't speak of it. She can't speak of it. She can hardly think of it. So she doesn't. She just sits on the step, allowing herself to rest between chores, and watch the children run.

The children slow as they approach her, their dark eyes bright. From their raiment, she guesses that at least two of the little ones are pilgrims, country-dwellers who have come to Jerusalem for the Passover celebration, but the lead boy is city bred. He has that look, although in the three weeks since they've arrived in Jerusalem, she has not seen him before nor did she recall him from their visits in the past.

The littlest one is a girl, a tiny child with a heart-shaped face and her hair neatly tucked up in her veil. The sight of her unexpectedly hurts—like a dagger to the heart, so Dinah looks away.

The children are slow now, catching their breath, though their leader still shouts, "He is here!"

Overhead, a shutter flies up and Hannah's irritated voice cuts through their exaltation: "What *is* this racket! Who has come?"

The boy pauses and looks up. He is so close to Dinah that she can make out the fine embroidery that lines his tunic and the long lashes that frame his mischievous eyes. He is strong and confident—a leader already and he is proud to proclaim the news: "The Nazarene! He is come!"

A littler boy in gray pipes up: "The King of the Jews! He is *here*!"

It should be a momentous announcement.

Another day. Another messiah, Dinah thinks.

Every ten or fifteen years or so, there has been one crackpot or another claiming to be the messiah, the returning Moses, come to throw the Romans out and restore the House of David. Insanity, mostly, not in themselves to be blamed. Some were thought to be possessed, but Dinah is too world-weary to be easily convinced of that. There are enough things in this world that break the spirit and the mind. You do not need to look for the supernatural.

The only remarkable thing is how *many* self-proclaimed messiahs there have been in the past few years. Five this year alone, to her knowledge, but probably three times as many. There have been enough for even her quiet husband to remark, "Messiahs sure have been in season lately."

So Dinah is not impressed. But it is a different story for the usually crotchety Hannah, who, for once, does not immediately scold.

"Jesus of Nazareth?" she asks and now Dinah looks up. Old Hannah is leaning out the window, her chin jutted out and a brightness in her eyes, looking like she's seeing the coming of Elijah himself in the small boy.

And then she says *it*.

"The one who survived the purge?" old Hannah asks.

"Yes!" the boy responds. Now his gaze shifts to Dinah, who sits as though turned into stone on the doorstep. "He came in on a donkey and they laid a carpet of branches for Him. He's *here*! He's *finally come*."

With that, he is off, running down the alleyway as though all of the joy of heaven propels him along. His voice is sing-song as he runs with renewed vigor, the children chasing after him, laughing, joying radiating out of their small bodies.

"He is here, He has come!"

Their high, clear voices ring throughout the alleyway, filling the air with their happiness. It is so present that Dinah can almost see it. But their excitement doesn't touch her. She has been struck to the heart—she is numb.

He has come.

The one who survived the purge.

Dinah sits on the doorstep and wishes that she could shrivel away into nothingness.

2

The Dream

That night, Dinah dreams.

She is in Bethlehem again, in their tiny quarters, and it is night. It is swelteringly hot and still, made worse because she's closed the shutters and sits in the dark. She clutches the baby to her chest and feels Anne squirming in protest. *Don't cry,* she prays. *Don't cry.*

Oh, how Dinah prays.

Outside, in the night, she hears the cracking of smashed wood, the shrieks of women and children, and the wailing and protests of the men.

One of the servant girls, whose name she does not know, had come only moments earlier, banging on Dinah's door.

"*They are coming! They are coming for the children.*"

Such things seemed impossible—pogroms are barbaric, not something that happens here, now, under the umbrella of civilized Rome. Anyway, according to the official record, the purge never happened. The incident in Bethlehem—it diminishes with each official report—was later explained away as an act of terrorism, local hoodlums venting their spleens. The governor swore to find the perpetrators. To the surprise of absolutely no one, he was unable to find them.

That night, Dinah tells herself, *It's impossible. It happened in Egypt. It cannot happen here.*

But she hears the proof of the girl's proclamation echoing down the street. Cries and wailing and the smashing of wooden doors, coming closer and closer. She is alone in the house with her child—Jacob is away on business—and as she presses back harder and harder into the wall, it becomes clear that she has to make decision right now: flee or hide?

Dinah never can remember what made her decide to stay. What made her douse the lights and pray that they would pass over her dwelling, thinking it empty. She has tormented herself endlessly for not slipping out under the cover of darkness, running away down the alleys and hiding until the danger has passed. But Bethlehem wasn't home—they were only there for the census—and there was no assurance that the neighbors wouldn't turn her in. Fear has made traitors and villains before and since.

Perhaps even then, she did not really, *truly* believe the warning. This is Bethlehem, not some barbarian land. The Romans are not liked, to be sure, but the deal has been clear: Hebrew subjection for security. *Pax Romana.*

Surely someone would come—surely someone would save them. Surely, she would be spared.

The sounds grow louder—men shouting. Women crying. Children screaming.

They are approaching.

Dinah begs the dream version of herself, *Leave, leave, please, please, leave!*

But the nightmare stays true to the reality, and she remains.

The sound of the shouting grows louder. She can hear the men kicking in Abigail's door, the pleading of Abigail's rabbi husband as they knock him down to get inside. Their daughter, Tamar, screaming—then a baby's shriek—a shriek that is cut short with the suddenness of a knife thrust.

They are coming for the children...

Cold fear washes over her. She knows, dimly, that this is a dream, but this realization makes the agony worse—she knows what is about to happen. She knows that her house is next. She clutches Anne to her and hears the small mew of protest. She tries to calm herself, hoping that by stilling herself, Anne will also still. But Anne is waking up. She stretches, opens her perfect little mouth in an O.

She's awake. She starts to fuss.

They will not kill her—they only want the boys. Pharaoh only wanted the males.

But this is not reassuring.

Anne makes a squawking sound. It is so dark that Dinah cannot see her own hand, let alone her daughter's face. But she knows that squawk. She knows the little screwed up face Anne is making. She's hungry. She's hot. She is about to cry.

Then, suddenly, the men are outside Dinah's door. They shout. They pound on the door. The latch rattles.

Dinah presses herself back against the stone wall. Anne fights her grip. Belatedly, Dinah realizes what to do—she loosens her robes, tries to force her shaking fingers to work, to bring her infant to her breast. Anne is shaking too, with barely repressed rage and frustration.

No!

"No one home?" someone outside asks.

As if in answer, Anne wails.

Dinah screams. The door bursts open and the men, bloody daggers in their hands, storm in. The light from their torches dazzles her, stabbing her eyes. The men are dressed like bandits, but they move like soldiers. Half of them stagger from drink. She can see their eyes, feel their evil. She screams and she pleads. She covers Anne with her own body.

"No, no, no! She– She—!"

She can't choke out the words, *she's a girl!*

Dinah is thrown aside, kicking and fighting. Anne is ripped from her arms.

Dinah turns in time to see the slayer, holding her daughter, both illuminated by the torch light.

Anne squirms in one arm, her little hand batting uselessly.

The man holds Anne in one hand and a dagger in the other.

The hand with the dagger rises and falls.

There is an arc of blood.

The little bundle falls.

All sound stops.

All time stops.

Then the men have gone, and Dinah is alone in the house. Alone with the bundle and Anne's blood, warm and crimson, staining the walls and the floor. It's everywhere. It stains the blanket, the little embroidered gown, the tiny face and the still hands, Dinah's own hands as they shakenly try to revive the girl.

Anne's screaming has stopped.

Dinah's echoes.

She is still screaming when Jacob wakes her. He folds her into his arms, his deep voice soothing in her ear.

"You're safe, my darling. You're safe."

She grips him for dear life. She doesn't *feel* safe. All those years and still, she feels a deep sense of insecurity, as though at any moment, at any time, anyone might beat down the door.

It is nonsense, this feeling and she knows it. She clings to Jacob, relishing his strength and asks the same question she always asks, the one that haunts her, the one that can never be answered: "Why?"

His grip on her tightens.

"The Lord only knows," he says.

Dinah knows this. For years, she's pleaded with the Lord for answers. But He has never seen fit to reply . No matter how she sobbed and how much she begged, the Lord remained silent. In retaliation, her heart hardened.

They'd wanted a big family, the pair of them. They'd suffered through miscarriage after still birth. Only Anne had survived, but she'd been enough. Enough until she was taken and Dinah was left with only tears and questions.

Why?

One day, she stopped crying. She stopped asking. And she vowed never to beg again.

Even now, her anger staggers her. The dream is as fresh and real as it had been when it was no dream. Time and familiarity has not dulled the edge. She releases Jacob, tells him to sleep.

"I'm all right now," she says. She even believes it.

Still, the dream, the nightmare, the memory, is so strong that it takes an hour before she stops shaking.

The Invitation

The day has been peaceful and calm. Dinah has had the house to herself for the morning and a good part of the afternoon, too. Even Jacob was absent. He had business all day with his cousins and acquaintances, as was normal when they came to Jerusalem, and would probably bring some business associate home for dinner. Dinah cooks for twelve, just in case, and wishes that they could afford their own, private residence while in Jerusalem.

Almost as soon as she thinks this, she feels ungrateful. Silas and his wife are always wonderful hosts and never miss an opportunity to make them feel welcome. Silas is like a brother to Jacob—childhood friends, he can make Jacob laugh like a child again. Rebecca, when she isn't pregnant or attending to her numerous, also fertile sisters, is a trifle pompous, but a hard worker and a gracious hostess. She would never have allowed Dinah to lift a finger, except that Dinah insisted on doing so to allow the maid some well-earned time off.

"I grow fat and lazy when I'm here," she had said to Rebecca. "I need work."

In a household as large as Rebecca's, there is always work to be done, even with the most efficient maids, and Rebecca is has too much on her plate to turn away offered help.

Cooking is soothing for Dinah—it is easier on her eyes than her acclaimed embroidery work and it allows her to take control of a space in the house. But more than that, the act of feeding her family and friends, in some ways, fills a nameless void within her. Of all the work she does, it is the most satisfying. If she had been more faithful, she might have even said that it approached a spiritual act. But Dinah would never presume on theology.

So she cooks and gradually the family refills the house. The boys return first, full of energy after a day of Torah studies, history, and math. The girls are also in school, though they have additional studies of sewing and the womanly arts. Dinah often wonders why Rebecca hasn't kept the girls home with her. A clever woman like Rebecca could surely teach them all they need and not suffer from their absence. But Rebecca is a much younger woman than Dinah and has always been more ambitious. Home is where she sleeps—Jerusalem, with its market stalls and her numerous rental properties and political connections and high-class society is her true home.

All of Rebecca's children stop in to say hello to Dinah, sniffing at the pots and complaining of hunger.

"I'm always glad when you cook," Gad tells her, looking earnestly into the oven. "You cook the bestest."

He hugs her around the waist before he skips off to play with his brothers.

Dinah loves them dearly.

The eldest daughter, Leah, is fast approaching womanhood and knows that a young man has already been scouted for her, although she does not know which. Dinah can sense her nervousness when she stops by to say hello. In previous years, Leah had been calm, an older sister who knew her place in the world. But now, in the awkward stretch between identities, the surety of her youth has given place to an equally natural feeling of displacement.

Dinah remembers this feeling, although time and distance have had their effect. She remembered the days of her engagement, the long, seemingly endless time between their vows and the beginning of their marriage and living together. She remembers the awkwardness mixed with high hopes and dreams for a big family and prosperous life. She remembers, too, the slow dawning realization that not all dreams are meant for reality. But she shoves those thoughts away and smiles at Leah, who asks a question about seasoning.

Leah does not know who she is yet, Dinah thinks. But she will learn. Once she is married, she will learn.

She answers Leah's question and then the girl is called away to a game with the younger girls. Dinah sees the relief in her motions as she runs off—the games are familiar. She knows what she is about there.

Dinah is looking forward to a quiet night with the family, although with such a large brood, *quiet* is not what normally happens. Like Leah, she likes knowing where she is and what her place is. She likes being useful. She likes cooking and feeling as though she belongs to the larger household, even in a small subservient way. It is better than the jealousy that often torments her and the sorrow that will, even now, attempt to swallow her whole.

Despite Dinah's own ambivalence towards God, Passover has become more meaningful over the years. Celebrating here, in Jerusalem, in the midst of the political and theological unrest that grows more and more dangerous each year, is a reminder of God's peace. Just as their enslaved ancestors in Egypt ate in safety during a dark night of death and sorrow, so their ancestors break bread in the midst a Roman occupation.

So when Rebecca comes home, breathless and glowing with excitement to tell her that they will all be going out that night, Dinah is not pleased.

"I have already made dinner," she protests.

"We will bring some with us, to share," Rebecca says. She is flying about the kitchen, pulling out baskets, linen, and loaves of bread. "Martha will appreciate that."

"Martha?"

"She's hosting. You know Martha. Hosting always turns her into a nervous wreck. With that sister of hers, you can hardly blame her, although I've heard that she's been turning over a new leaf..."

Dinah knows of Martha and Mary and their brother and the rumors that have been swirling about them. Martha is an unmarried domestic tyrant, Lazarus is a hard worker but frequently ill, and as for Mary... Well, to speak of her reputation was unkind.

But it is not the thought of this strange little triplet that makes Dinah feel suddenly trapped and uneasy, like there's a band slowly tightening on her chest. They were, for all their faults, merely ordinary Hebrews, and even now were remarkable for only one thing: their association with the Nazarene.

Rebecca is exclaiming over the food—"It smells and is delicious!"—while pulling out clay pots to travel with.

"I tried to convince old Hannah to watch the children," she is saying. "But she was so excited about coming with us that I didn't have the heart to ask."

"She should go!" Dinah says, relieved to find a voice and an excuse. "I'll stay with them."

"Nonsense. You *must* hear the teacher, Dinah. Leah can watch the children." She pulls out a travel pot that has some decorative relief on it and studies it assiduously. It is a little too small for such a gathering, Dinah knows. But it is pretty and a little more expensive than the others. Rebecca isn't an especially frivolous woman, but she and Silas had done well, and one could not blame them for wanting to show off a little.

She puts the pot on the table and bends once more in search of others. "You must go—Silas and Jacob are coming home early to come with us."

She pulls up a larger, plainer pot and stands upright, turning to smile at Dinah. "I've heard Him once before. He is..."

"Another messiah?" Dinah asks, bitterly.

Rebecca winces, as though the words struck her.

"He is... different," she says.

The words pour out of Dinah before she can stop them: "Aren't they all, every one of them? Different and ready to save us from all threats, from the Romans to cimex?"

There's a sudden stillness. Rebecca looks at Dinah with caution and curiosity. Dinah feels mean—she has sucked all the joy out of the room.

Even so, she does not apologize. They had all been taken in, at one point or another. She had no intention of being taken in by *Him*, by the Nazarene of all people.

Lord, I cannot. I cannot!

Rebecca places the pot on the table carefully and then folds her hands across her stomach. She is pondering.

Dinah waits.

The room has gone silent, but all around them, sounds of life permeate the walls—the girls giggling in one room, the boys reciting in another, the busy street along the front. Aramaic, Egyptian, and Arabic mingle in a cross-section of peoples, all ancient enemies, trying to get along, trying to buy, sell, and live. Like a whiplash, they hear the strident tone of the noon-day patrol, the guards marching through the streets, the newest oppressor in a long line of bullies, killers, pagans, and despots, speaking in their crisp northern Latin.

It is a chilling reminder of how perilous their world still is.

It feels to Dinah as though the world were trying to beat in and get them. Perhaps Rebecca feels the same, for she turns suddenly and pulls the shutters closed against the street. The sounds of the outdoors fade but are still present. Nevertheless, in the sudden darkness, Dinah feels better.

Rebecca lingers a minute, her back to Dinah. She appears to be trying to decide upon something. Dinah stands where she is, feeling more like a girl of Leah's age than the married woman of property and age that she is. The feeling remains when Rebecca turns, her mind made up.

"I know what you mean about the other messiahs," she says slowly. "I have no wish to listen to charlatans. But this man..."

She hesitates, and Dinah steels herself for the inevitable excuses: "*He's different... He's the real thing... He's truly a man of God...*" and of course, "*He is only collecting for the poor, not himself!*"

But when Rebecca speaks, she does not say any of those things. She says, "I think you ought to come, Dinah. I won't insist. But... you ought to come and just listen. That's all. Life is a burden, sister. Heavier for you than most, I know. He makes it easier. I don't know how or even how to explain it. I just know that..." She shrugs. "He does."

There is something in the way that Rebecca speaks. A stillness, perhaps, a surety. The look in her eye is unsettling—she looks so peaceful, so sure, so *right* that there is a strength in her that would have been frightening had it not also been cloaked in something kind, something loving, something so fiercely strong that all arguments would fail on contact.

It is not what Dinah was expecting to see or hear. Those who follow the messiahs are zealots, angry and forceful or, worse, so much in love with their savior that they lose all sense of self and reason.

Rebecca has not lost herself. In fact, in speaking, she seemed more like her own self than Dinah can ever recall seeing. For this Rebecca was not desperate or trying to gain anything. She was, to all practical intents and purposes, just speaking the truth.

Dinah doesn't know what to make of this. And though she desperately does not want to see this man, this Nazarene, though her stomach twists and something deep within her screams that the pain would not be sustainable, that it would wound her beyond repair, she finds herself saying, "Bring the decorative pot. I'll carry another so there will be enough food for all."

Rebecca's smile lights the darkened room.

4

The Servant

The Teacher is late.

Martha's house is filled to capacity, hot and teeming with chatter and thinly veiled impatience. People want their blessings. They want to hear Him. They want to be able to tell their friends, "I sat at His feet! The one who raised Jairus' daughter!"

Dinah helps Martha serve them. She has long ago learned that the best way to remain invisible at parties is to assist with the food. And it works. Her husband is in the corner, talking with a group of his business associates. Rebecca is talking about children with a group of her friends. Old Hannah is holding court among her elderly friends, all comparing aches and pains and family dramas. They all have forgotten her, which is well, for they might make her mingle. Dinah is here only as a favor to her hostess. Beyond that courtesy, she feels no obligation.

So she works. And she listens. As she passes plates around, or refills glasses, she hears snippets of conversations and she learns more about the people that have crowded this space to see Him. They are restless and bright with anticipation and anxiety. They brag, but with one ear always towards the door. They are nervous and excited and there is a frisson of danger in the atmosphere.

A certain level of anxiety is to be expected. After all, this is occupied Jerusalem on the eve of the highest of holy nights, and the city is teaming with outsiders, insiders, malcontents, zealots, rebels, soldiers, and the easily misled. But the tension in Martha's house is...different.

Dinah is unsure why. Openly, the guests worry that He would not come after all. "He is," they whisper, "unpredictable in His way." They speak of that time when He disappeared from the crowds, only to be discovered across the Red Sea. The crowds had followed Him and He taught, but He has a habit, not only of disappearing, but of speaking in riddles.

"He preaches peace," one man says, "but the Pharisees want war."

Those gathered here fear that this gathering is not important enough for His attention. One woman, who hardly looks at Dinah as Dinah re-fills her glass, murmurs to her friend, "He might even be casting out another-"

"Don't even say it!" the terrified friend says.

Beneath the current of cheerful chatter and polite conversation, the guests worry. They drink. And they stew.

Dinah serves and she listens. But while there is security in her anonymity, she is not spared. Women are everywhere in Martha's house. They are drawn to the Teacher, like flies to honey, and some of them have brought gifts of food and clothing for Him and the band of fishermen and tax collectors that He has collected. But though they wait for Him, they speak of other things.

"...I just don't know what to do with my Hadassah," complains one woman as she plucks grapes from Dinah's tray. "She is such a plain girl. Took after her father's side, I'm afraid."

"Try raising a houseful of boys," says Judith, sardonically. "You'll thank the Creator for your plain girl."

Judith is plain herself, but blessed with a rich husband and six boys, riches that she finds every opportunity to rub into the faces of her friends and acquaintances. They are used to her, however, so it is probably only Dinah who feels the sting of rebuke. A wife is supposed to be not only faithful and industrious, but fruitful. By and large, every woman in this room has done her duty or is in the process of it. They speak of their children with a glow of pride, even the pregnant woman who is complaining about her swollen feet to Rebecca.

"It is a small price to pay," Rebecca says as Dinah passes within earshot, "for the blessing. Your husband must be so pleased."

The pregnant woman's face softens into an expression of glowing pride.

"Jeremiah is beside himself," she confesses and lifts her hand to show off the bracelet he'd given her in celebration of their new family.

All around the room, it is the same—talk of the Teacher, talk of the children. Every word is like a spear to Dinah's heart. She feels isolated. She feels like a leper, ringing a bell to warn the others away. She feels unseen and forgotten. As she goes into the kitchen to swap the now-empty tray for a pitcher of watered down wine, she wishes with all her heart that she could just slip out the back door and run all the way back home.

But she can't. For many reasons, among which is the fact that a harried and wild-haired Martha is hastily slicing bread and blocking the back door with her body.

"I am so grateful for you, Dinah," she says, wiping her forehead. "It is so difficult to play hostess all alone."

She says this in her familiar, distinctly martyred tone.

It is a not strictly true statement—besides Martha and Dinah, the kitchen hums with the movement of servants, girls who have been sent to Martha to learn how to run a household. They are meek and well-trained, efficient enough to be left alone to the task, if Martha were the type of woman who *could* leave things alone.

Dinah knows that Martha is not thinking of the servant girls—she is thinking of her wayward sister, Mary, who even now sits in the outer room as though a guest herself.

There is much that has been said on the situation. But Dinah only says, "Of course. I am pleased to help," and slips outside before she has to endure another tirade about ungrateful profligate relatives.

I must not become bitter like her, she thinks, as she wends through the crowd, refilling goblets.

A nasty thought replies, *You won't, for aren't you Rebecca's charity?*

The very idea takes her breath away. Hardly has it processed when she hears Judith saying, "And my Rachel is already expecting my first grandchild!"

Judith's back is to Dinah, her hand, holding an empty goblet extended towards her. She is waiting, without looking, for Dinah to fill it. The other women, politely congratulating Judith on her good fortune, also do not look. They do not see her. They hardly even note the pitcher of wine, so wrapped are they in their own affairs.

Bitterness falls over Dinah like a suffocating cloak. She has an instinct to pour the contents of her pitcher all over Judith, to smash the clay jar against the wall and storm out in a swirl of robes and dignity.

Fortunately for the expectant grandmother, Dinah hears Jacob's laughter and remembers herself. She thinks of Jacob and Rebecca. She thinks, *You wanted to be invisible.*

She pours wine into Judith's glass and hurries away.

5

The Woman

There is one spot in Martha's house where anxiety about the Teacher or anything else seems not to touch. Ironically, it is where Martha's sister, Mary, lounges.

Mary is a pretty girl, long-limbed and bright-eyed and with a sort of wild courage that is often stirred for the wrong reasons. She sits, in her indolent way, among a grouping of other women, dressed as carelessly as it is rumored that she lives her life. By her side this evening is, of all things, a small perfume jar, delicately painted. She touches this constantly, as though to reassure herself that it is still there. Why she brought it here, to this gathering space, is anyone's guess.

She is a difficulty, this Mary. A lost soul and a blight on her more steady—if more rigid—sister's reputation. Dinah has met her once before and did not like her then. She is not inclined to change her opinion now, even though the girl has changed, somehow. Her manners are steadier, and her eyes, when they briefly meet Dinah's, are calmer, more thoughtful, and she is altogether quieter, more sure. And there is the fact that Mary is seated amongst, not the frivolous young things as had been her wont before, but among matrons. She converses with ease, as if she were not a head-strong, heedless, unmarried embarrassment, rather as though she were... well, one of them.

It is a wonder, truly, and Dinah longs to comment on it. However, one can hardly mention it without being rude and there is no one to confide in, anyway. So Dinah tucks her wonderment away and approaches Mary's circle with her pitcher of wine.

Mary is talking avidly to the older woman dressed in blue, who sits on a bench in front of her. The woman on the bench is still and peaceful. Mary, by contrast, is animated and her voice low even though her speech is rapid fire. She stops when Dinah pauses next to them and offers to refill their goblets.

Some of the women instantly accept—one women in an elaborately embroidered shawl practically shoves her goblet into Dinah's face. The woman on the bench demurs.

Dinah fills the pro-offered cups and turns to Mary to do the same—there is not one person in this room who *hasn't* heard stories of the young woman's ability to drink grown men under the table. To her shock, Mary hesitates.

"I..." she says, her eyes dropping to her hands, where the goblet is still half full. Then: "No, thank you. This is enough for me."

This surprises Dinah. It shocks the woman in the embroidered shawl—her mouth drops open. Nearly everyone in this little group is surprised, including Mary herself, who falters and looks up at Dinah with something like an appeal in her eyes.

The only one who is not surprised is the woman on the bench. She leans forward to pat Mary's hand. The veil falls back a little to reveal the face of a woman about Dinah's age, ordinary in appearance, with a warm smile and a touch of gray in the few hairs that escape her coverings.

Mary grasps the older woman's hand gratefully.

"Thank you," she says, and, forgetting herself, in a flash of her old ways, bends down and kisses the woman's hand.

The woman laughs. "Oh, child," she says and turns to Dinah to smile her own refusal. "Thank you. I have enough."

Her words are warm and her smile kind and worn. This woman looks much like any other Jewish mother in Jerusalem: brown eyes, graying hair, worry-lines spidering across her face. She is dressed neatly, but without fuss. There is nothing about her that would draw attention except for the calm, the peace, that seems to emanate from her like rays from the sun. Dinah feels...warm and peaceful, a feeling that is familiar and maternal, like being in her own mother's embrace. Like being at home, for the first time in decades.

All of this and yet she doesn't not know this woman.

The moment expands and holds, then breaks. The woman is drawn back into her conversation with the others, Mary still holding on to her hand.

For a moment, Dinah stands there, bereft and baffled. An intense longing to sit here, to listen, to bathe in the warm glow of the comradery, overwhelms and frightens her. Before she can move, a familiar voice breaks into her reverie.

"Ladies, would you like some bread?"

Martha is there, holding a tray of fresh-baked bread drizzled with olive oil and spices. She beams with pride, all her attention trained on the woman on the bench. Even the presence of her wayward, lazy sister, doesn't distract her—Martha's focus is so intense that she sees nothing else until the woman on the bench takes a slice of the bread and declares it delicious.

Martha looks as if she could explode with pride.

Mary, next to the woman in blue, reaches and takes a large slice before the other guests have had a chance. Martha's eyes narrow.

The elder sister opens her mouth to scold, and Dinah, aware of the eyes of the other women upon them, intervenes.

"Anna, you *must* try Martha's bread," she says. She takes Martha's arm with the tray and gently extends it to the other women. They eagerly snatch at the contents. A chorus of praise – "So salty!" "So light!" "You must tell me how you made this, Martha!" – fills the air. Martha is distracted and flattered and the crisis is averted.

Once the women in the corner have had their share of the bread, Dinah steers Martha towards the other guests. She stays with Martha, filling people's cups as they snatch at the tray. Martha is a shield—where she goes, people do not speak of anything other than the food she offers or the wine that Dinah pours.

But even as she works, Dinah is aware of the woman on the bench, chatting quietly with Mary and the others. The women listen intently, as though to a teacher. Perhaps the woman is a teacher or a prophet, maybe; one of the women who are constantly in the temple, interceding for their race.

It's possible: this woman is the only person in the room completely at peace.

Dinah wonders what that must feel like.

When the tray is empty, Martha turns to Dinah and says, "When *is* He coming?" in a tone of impatience. No matter how good the food or plentiful the wine, the night will not be a success if the man of honor does not arrive.

When Dinah doesn't respond to Martha's question, her hostess follows her gaze across the room towards Mary and the woman on the bench. Martha's face pinches up again.

"Honestly, I do my best for her, never complain, never demand, and look at her. Just look at her. My sister. Makes me glad I never married and had children. We've been spared one burden anyway, haven't we, Dinah?"

She grins at Dinah as though they are conspirators, outsmarting the world.

Rage flares up within Dinah. *I am* not *like you! I did* not *choose this!*

She can hardly swallow the anger and knows if she does not say something, Martha will sense her wrath. So, she gestures with the pitcher.

"Who is that woman your sister talks with?" she asks. "She seems..."

She doesn't know how to finish the sentence. Familiar? Unusual? Peaceful? None of these seem right.

Martha glances and her face softens.

"Oh," she says. "That is Mary. The mother of the Nazarene."

The world stops. All noise is suspended except for the pounding of Dinah's heart.

Distantly, Martha continues, "She's a widow now and a holy woman." Martha steps in closer, her voice dropping. "Did you hear about the purge? *She* was there. Herod wanted Him dead, so she and her husband had to flee into Egypt. They only barely escaped." She sighs and shakes her head. "Can you even imagine?"

Dinah can't move. She can't breathe. She can't speak. She feels a thousand invisible claws, tear-ing at her heart, her lungs, her throat. She knows if she even blinks, she'll either attack Martha or tear the room apart with her screaming.

Martha, her tormentor, doesn't even notice. In fact, she hardly finishes speaking when someone calls to her and she goes to them, leaving Dinah alone, trembling with rage and sorrow and injustice.

Across the room, Mary, *His* mother, glances around the room. The mother of the one who survived. The one who *caused* everything. The one who ended Dinah's motherhood.

Rage builds. Anger roars. Pain screams silently.

Dinah turns on her heel and flees.

6

The Christache is pounding through her veins.

How dare she? How dare *she!*

Dinah slips through the kitchen door, past the startled kitchen help. Her hip connects with a basket, sending it and the contents rolling across the floor. She barely notices.

"Can you even imagine?"

Yes, Martha, I bloody well can…

Her hands are shaking so hard she can hardly grasp the door handle. She doesn't see the look on the faces of the servants. She doesn't hear Martha calling for her, confused. She sees only the door and flashes from the past:

Anne's tiny hand, gripping her blouse.

The rough feeling of the wall, pressing into her back as she tries to hide.

The flash of the torches.

The arc of the blood.

"Can you even imagine?"

His mother had been there. She'd survived. He'd survived. And God had allowed her to watch Him grow. Mary had been a mother, while Dinah had only ever been a tragedy.

Why? WHY?

Martha's door slams behind Dinah.

She is outside in the warm, still air.

Unlike the crush of the street in front of the house, the alleyway in the back is dark and still. Night wraps around her like a cloak. Dinah is seething, raging, too upset to even notice that she is alone, in a dark city, a Hebrew woman, a target, a victim in the making. She turns and stalks down the alleyway, her sandled feet hitting the uneven pavement like fists pounding into a wall.

"She was there!"

That woman was there. Her Son, the cause of it all. The Man they'd come to see—the reason why Anne had died, why Dinah's hopes and dreams had withered and died too.

Why?

"*She was* there."

Anne died. Why did she? Why didn't He?

She hears an infant wail and in her distress, she doesn't know if it's a real child or Anne's voice, haunting her now as it has so often haunted her dreams. Dinah breaks into a run, her hands balled into fists.

My child. Why? Why?

She'd been a good Jewess. She'd prayed and fasted and hoped. She'd asked for only one thing. She'd endured miscarriage after miscarriage to get it.

She'd had Anne for one brief moment in time.

And then *He* came and brought the killers with Him.

Hate courses through her veins.

Oh, Anne. Why, God, why? What had I ever done to You? Why?

Dinah runs but the pain keeps pace.

Then it happens.

It's so dark and she is running so fast that, when the alley curves, Dinah is not prepared. She thrusts her hands up only just in time to save her face.

Her body crashes into the bricks. Pain, real, physical pain, crushes the breath out of her chest. Lights flash before her eyes. She stumbles back, vaguely aware of voices, male voices, and hands, male hands, touching her shoulders, calling out to her.

"Are you all right?"

She is outside. Alone, unescorted, unprotected, in Jerusalem. She's done what only the most foolish women do. Her eyes are watering from the blow—she can't even see the men, just hear them, feel them. The flashes of torches bring on panic and she lashes out.

She thinks, *Jacob is going to be so angry.*

Then she thinks, *I don't care. Let them do what they will.*

The fear and anger die swiftly. She buries her face in her hands. Someone pushes her back until she is leaning, sagging, against a wall.

Anne. Oh, my little Anne!

The men's voices blend into a cacophony.

"...drunk..."

"She's hurt."

"Is she possessed?"

"...punched at me..."

"Oh, hush, Matthew..."

Then, in the middle of a sentence, she catches a word: "...Teacher..."

The shock of the word brings her out of herself. She lowers her hands and looks at the men surrounding her.

They are a disparate lot. A few hold lanterns, others are clutching their cloaks to their chests as though concealing weapons. Some are old, one very young, hardly more than a boy. Some are wealthy but most are not. She recognizes Simon, a big fisherman who is somehow related to Rebecca, but it is clear that he doesn't know her, for he keeps looking around, as though expecting an ambush at any moment.

He is more afraid than I am, she thinks.

The thought is vaguely funny.

The youngest of them says again, "Teacher?"

Through the group of men, the Teacher appears.

Later, Dinah would come to wonder *how* it was that she picked the Teacher, the Nazarene, out of a crowd of strange men. People would ask, "Was it His demeanor? His bearing? His looks?"

There was no answer.

In truth, there is nothing about Him that stands out. He is dressed as the others, walks like them, His accent, when He speaks, is just like Simon's, with only the slightest of country accents to distinguish from the city men. He looks like any other man.

All the same, Dinah knows Him at once. As He approaches, she draws herself up off of the wall, shakes her shoulders free of the helping hands, and glares at the Man.

The Nazarene stands before her, flanked by His group. His face is lit by the lamps and His dark eyes are focused on her. He is thin and dressed simply, His tunic trimmed in a simple, masculine version of the embroidery that his mother wore. He is young. In His thirties. The same age that Anne would have been.

The same age that Anne *should* have been.

Anger surges like the ocean in the midst of a storm. It drives Dinah forward.

"You," she hisses and glares up at Him. "It's *you!*"

Simon's head whips around at her tone. He steps closer, but a slight gesture from the Teacher stops him from coming closer.

"I am," the Teacher says.

His voice is low and gentle, but there is strength in it. Dinah becomes aware of power, shuddering through the air around them, like lightning in a storm, only more dangerous, more focused. She knows, even as her glare intensifies, that she is stepping into a lion's den. But she can't stop herself. Pain, injustice, rage, all cry out of justice, scream for it, dying for it. It is this that drives her to move even closer, even as the warning bells clang in her head.

The Teacher watches her.

She is close enough to see that He is tired. His cheeks are hollow and He looks as though He is experiencing torment Himself.

Good, she thinks. *Feel it.*

He says, "What do you have to do with me, daughter?"

The term irritates her. She snaps, "I am *not* your daughter. I am a mother. *My* child died. My child died for *you!* In Bethlehem. They wanted you. *You* ran away and I— My—"

Suddenly, she cannot speak. Her throat closes. She cannot breathe, the rage and sorrow is too great. Anne's cries ring in her ears.

But He—He is still.

"Why?" Dinah finally whispers. And then again, begging: "Why?"

She cannot hold His gaze any longer. Her eyes drop, her hands press to her mouth. She is hiccupping, hard and painful, close to heaving. Her head pounds. Her body begins to shut down. Her knees buckle and her strength gives way—she begins to fall.

A hand grasps her elbow and holds her up.

Strength surges through her at the touch. She reaches out, grips His sleeve. When she lifts her head, the Teacher is gazing at her with such a look of sorrow that her own grief seems like a drop in a vast ocean.

"I know," the Nazarene says softly. "She is safe. She is home with my Father."

There is sorrow, yes. But there is something else here too. Something too vast for Dinah to recognize, a thing so obvious, so natural, that she cannot name it. It is as ancient as time itself and as fresh as the tear that drops onto her cheek.

Then He speaks again:

"She died for me. And I will die for her."

Something rips free deep inside of Dinah. It is as though some part of her soul, long locked and chained in a cold dark place, has been set free. Sorrow is washed away by a strong current of joy. Warmth floods her—she experiences a *rightness* that she has never felt in her whole life.

Despite everything: wanting to hate Him and His mother, all the pain and the sorrow and the rage, without knowing why or how, Dinah recognizes the truth.

She recognizes Him.

She recognizes home.

Then, for the first time since that dark and terrible night in Bethlehem, Dinah weeps.

Afterword

This story is devoted to all women who have experienced the loss of a child - either through natural causes or abortion - or the inability to carry their own child.

You are seen.

You are loved.

You are not alone.

For non-judgmental support, please contact Catholic Charities or Project Rachel Ministries. People of all faiths – or no faith at all – are welcome.

Thank Yous

No story is written or published without support and inspiration from other people.

Many thanks to:

Xavier and Jonathan Garcia, whose short film "A Blood Throne" first inspired this story.

Pierre Rumpf, who thoughtfully invited me to a viewing of the film.

Angela and my mother, who read and wept over this story and encouraged me to publish it.

About the Author

Killarney Traynor lives in New Hampshire, where the long snowy winters give one plenty of time to come up with books and stories. She works as a bookkeeper by day and writes her stories at night and whenever time allows. When not writing, she can be found acting, directing, reading, traveling, or getting lost in Boston.

For more information or to learn more about other books she has written, please visit www.killarneytraynor.com

More Books